Kailee and the Frog Prince

by Diane Brookes

illustrated by Shelley Brookes

Raven Rock Publishing, Yellowknife, 1999

Text copyright © 1999 by Diane Brookes
Illustrations copyright © 1999 by Shelley Brookes
All rights reserved.
Published by Raven Rock Publishing,
21 Burwash Drive, Yellowknife NT X1A 2V1 CANADA

Canadian Cataloguing in Publication Data

Brookes, Diane.
  Kailee and the frog prince

  ISBN 0-9683640-2-0

  I. Brookes, Shelley, 1980-   II. Title.
PS8553.R6546K34 1999   jC813'.54   C99-910098-X
PZ7.B78978Ka 1999

Printed in Canada by Artisan Press Ltd. Yellowknife, Northwest Territories.

For the real Kailee,
without whom this story
would never have been
written, with love,
Aunty Diane.

Once upon a time there was a little girl named Kailee. She lived in an ordinary house in Ottawa, with a nice backyard to play in and a big old oak tree for climbing. Kailee had always thought her house and yard were just like every other house and yard but actually they were in a very magical place.

One summer day, Kailee decided to climb the big oak tree. One foot on the first branch, one foot on the next, step by step, hand by hand, she pulled herself up the tree by its big thick branches. When she reached the middle of the tree she found her favourite place to sit, surrounded by branches and big green oak leaves. Kailee loved this spot in the tree; a little green room all her own.

"I bet I could see my whole yard and my house from way up here," thought Kailee, and she reached forward and pulled apart the branches and the leaves. She looked down, then quickly let go of the branches. Surely she hadn't seen what she thought she saw. Once more, she pulled the branches apart and looked out. She squeezed her eyes shut, shook her head, and looked again. It was all still there.

What Kailee saw was not her own familiar house and yard, but a fairy tale place! Below her was a huge garden with beautiful flower beds and paths of paving stones running between them. In the sky birds flew and sang; over the flowers, butterflies fluttered. In the centre of the garden was a perfect lily pond. This was not her yard!

As she looked more closely she saw people
walking about on the paths. Kailee
recognized Snow White and her
prince; Beauty and the Beast;
Cinderella, who had lost her
shoe; and Mother Goose
with her arms full of
books.

Sitting beside the lily pond was a big frog wearing a little golden crown! The frog's mouth was moving. "Is he talking?" wondered Kailee.

Kailee scrambled down from the tree as quickly as she could. She ran over to the pond. Sure enough, the frog really was talking. In his croaky frog voice, he kept repeating, "I was a prince. I was a prince. I was a prince." Of course, thought Kailee, he must be the frog prince.

She began to explore the beautiful garden, wondering at everything she saw. As she came up to Cinderella, she stopped and said, very politely, "Excuse me, but can you please tell me where I am and how I can get back home?"

Cinderella ran past Kailee without so much as a glance or a word. Kailee was surprised.

She walked over to Beauty and her Beast and asked them, "Excuse me, but can you please tell me where I am and how I can get back home?"

Beauty and the Beast didn't seem even to notice Kailee but carried on their own conversation as before. Kailee started to feel afraid; she ran from one person to another asking her question but all the fairytale people looked right through her as if she wasn't even there and continued doing whatever they chose.

Finally Kailee ran back to the lily pond and the croaking frog. He was still repeating to himself, over and over, "I *was* a prince."

Kailee looked at the frog and asked once more, "Please tell me where I am and how I can get back home again."

The frog looked up at her, hopped a step closer and croaked, "I *was* a prince."

"I know," said Kailee, relieved that at least the frog seemed aware of her. "You're the frog prince and you are waiting for a princess to kiss you and break the spell."

The frog hopped closer, looked straight into her eyes and croaked, "I *could* be a prince."

"Yes, you could," Kailee agreed. "If only a princess will kiss you."

Once more the frog hopped closer. His big eyes looking imploringly into her own. "I *will* be a prince," he croaked.

"Me?" said Kailee, "you want *me* to kiss you? But I'm not a princess!"

"Again the frog croaked out his plea. Kailee looked down at the frog. He was a very big frog. His skin was green, wrinkled and slimy-looking. His eyes were big and bulgy and wet.

His mouth was huge and slobbery!

"Oh, I *couldn't!*" she replied.

Quietly, the frog asked again, "I *could* be a prince." He looked like he was crying, although his eyes were so wet already it was hard to be sure. Kailee looked at him again, at his sad, pleading eyes and said, "Oh, all right! But I'm not a princess, you know, so this probably won't work."

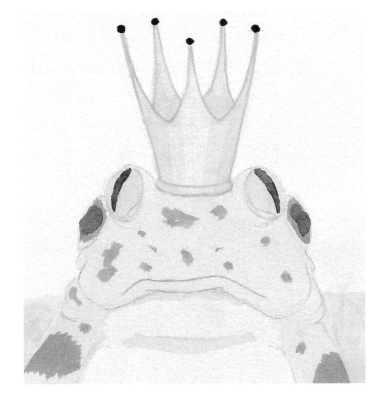

She leaned forward and picked up the frog in both hands. He felt just as awful as she had thought he would. She looked at the slobbery mouth, braced herself, closed her eyes tightly, leaned forward and kissed him.

With a magical noise the frog
jumped from her hands.

Kailee waited a moment and then opened first one eye and then the other. She stared about with amazement. She was back in her own yard beneath the oak tree. Gone were the flower beds and flagged paths; gone were the birds and butterflies; gone were the fairytale people; and gone was the frog. But in the grass at her feet something glittered.

Kailee knelt down and picked up a tiny golden crown and as she did, she heard, like a whisper carried on the wind,

"I was a prince. I could be a prince. I will be a prince. I AM a prince. Thaaaaank youuuuuuuuuuuuuuu............................"